R. Young

A Giant First-Start Reader

This easy reader contains only 43 different words, repeated often to help the young reader develop word recognition and interest in reading.

Basic word list for *Pussycat Kite*

a	his	pulls
across	hooray	runs
and	in	sail
blowing	into	sails
blows	is	sky
clouds	it	string
down	kite	tail
faster	long	the
fly	makes	today
gets	needs	too
goes	not	trouble
harder	now	up
has	Peter	will
help	Peter's	wind
higher		

Pussycat Kite

Written by Sharon Peters

Illustrated by Susan T. Hall

Troll Associates

Library of Congress Cataloging in Publication Data

Peters, Sharon.
    Pussycat kite.

    Summary: Peter, a cat, has a wonderful time flying his
kite one windy day, until a tree gets in the way.
        1. Children's stories, American.   [1. Kites—Fiction.
2. Cats—Fiction]   I. Hall, Susan, 1940-   ill.
II. Title.
PZ7.P44183Pu   1985   [E]   84-8632
ISBN 0-8167-0358-2 (lib. bdg.)

10   9   8   7   6   5   4   3   2   1

The wind is blowing today.

Hooray.

It blows the clouds across the sky.

It makes the clouds sail across the sky.

Peter has a kite.

Peter will fly his kite today.

His kite will fly across the sky.

His kite will sail across the sky.

Peter's kite has a long, long string.

It has a long, long tail, too.

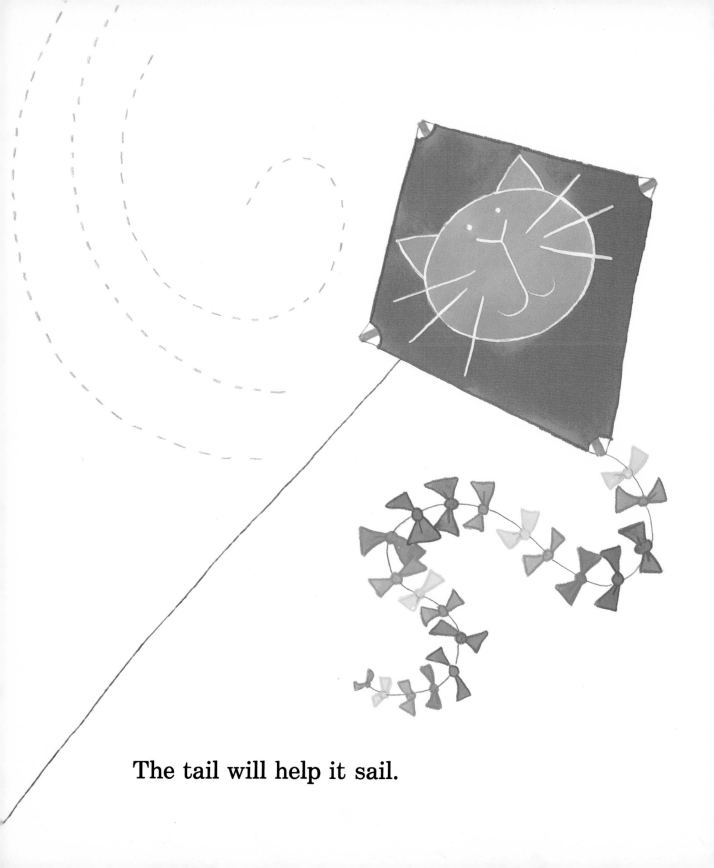

The tail will help it sail.

The tail will help it sail in the wind.

Peter runs into the wind.
The kite goes higher and higher.

Hooray.

Peter runs faster and faster.

The wind blows harder and harder.

Up, up, up goes the kite.
The wind blows harder.

The kite goes higher.

The kite runs into trouble!

The kite will not sail now.

Peter pulls the long, long string.

Peter's kite will not fly.
Peter needs help!

Peter gets help.

The kite sails down.

The wind blows.

The kite sails up.

Peter's kite sails across the sky!

Hooray.